D0573504

Commitment
^{to}Excellence

Compiled by
Katherine Karvelas
Successories, Inc., Editorial Coordinator

CAREER PRESS
3 Tice Road, P. O. Box 687
Franklin Lakes, NJ 07417
1-800-CAREER-1; 201-848-0310 (NJ and outside U. S.)
FAX: 201-848-1727

COMMITMENT TO EXCELLENCE
Cover design by Successories
Typesetting by Eileen Munson
Printed in the U.S.A. by Book-mart Press

To order this title, please call toll-free 1-800-CAREER-1 (NJ and Canada: 201-848-0310) to order using VISA or MasterCard, or for further information on books from Career Press.

Library of Congress Cataloging-in-Publication Data

Commitment to excellence : quotations that life the spirit toward
    excellence / by editors of Successories.
        p.   cm.
    ISBN 1-56414-387-2
    1. Achievement motivation--Quotations, maxims, etc.
 2. Excellence--Psychological aspects--Quotations, maxims, etc.
 I. Successories, Inc.
 BF503.C66   1998
 158.1--dc21   98-8600

Introduction

The search for personal and professional success is a lifelong journey of trial and error. This inspiring collection of wit and wisdom is a celebration of life's lessons. Each saying is a motivational push to stay on track of your goals and pursue your dreams.

In these pages you will find more than 300 powerful and compelling quotations from a diverse group of people—business professionals, writers, activists, actors, artists, sports professionals, scientists, philosophers, politicians, and everyday people who inspire us.

This unique collection was compiled after years of insightful reading and warm discussions with people who were kind enough to share their personal collections of quotations. Working on this book has been an enlightening and gratifying experience. We hope reading these quotes will be an equally gratifying and motivating experience for you on your journey of success.

Do not wish to be anything but
what you are, and try to be that
perfectly.

St. Francis de Sales

Well done is better than well said.

Ben Franklin

The difference between failure
and success is doing a thing nearly
right and doing a thing exactly
right.

Edward Simmons

The ultimate victory in a competition is derived from the inner satisfaction of knowing that you have done your best and that you have gotten the most out of what you had to give.

Howard Cosell

I am a big believer in the mirror test. All that matters is if you can look in the mirror and honestly tell the person you see there, that you've done your best.

John McKay

All glory comes from daring to begin.

Eugene F. Ware

Many of life's failures are men who did not realize how close they were to success when they gave up.

Anonymous

The distance doesn't matter; only the first step is difficult.

Madame du Deffand

Commitment
toExcellence

I do the best I know how, the very best I can; and I mean to keep on doing it to the end. If the end brings me out all right, what is said against me will not amount to anything. If the end brings me out all wrong, ten angels swearing I was right would make no difference.

Abraham Lincoln

Some men see things as they are and say "Why?" I dream things that never were, and say, "Why not?"

George Bernard Shaw

It's what you learn after you know it all that counts.

John Wooden

Success, in general, means the opportunity to experience and to realize the maximum forces that are within us.

David Sarnoff

The greatest thing in this world is
not so much where we are, but in
what direction we are moving.

Oliver Wendell Holmes

True greatness consists in being
great in little things.

Charles Simmons

The secret of success in life is
for a man to be ready for his
opportunity when it comes.

Benjamin Disraeli

Our chief want in life is somebody
who will make us do what we can.

Ralph Waldo Emerson

Do a little more each day than you
think you possibly can.

Lowell Thomas

You will become as small as your
controlling desire; as great as your
dominant aspiration.

James Allen

F*ar better it is to dare mighty things, to win glorious triumphs, even though checkered by failure, than to take rank with those poor spirits who neither enjoy nor suffer much, because they live in the grey twilight that knows neither victory nor defeat.*

Theodore Roosevelt

Anybody who accepts mediocrity—in school, on the job, in life—is a person who compromises, and when the leader compromises, the whole organization compromises.

Charles Knight

The price of success is hard work, dedication to the job at hand, and the determination that whether we win or lose, we have applied the best of ourselves to the task at hand.

Vince Lombardi

Great men are little men
expanded; great lives are ordinary
lives intensified.

Wilferd A. Peterson

It is quality rather than quantity
that matters.

Seneca

Discovery is seeing what everybody
else has seen, and thinking what
nobody else has thought.

Albert Szent-Gyorgi

Good is not good where better is expected.

Thomas Fuller

He who has put a good finish to his undertaking is said to have placed a golden crown to the whole.

Eustachius

Here is a simple but powerful rule: always give people more than they expect to get.

Nelson Boswell

I*f a man is called a streetsweeper,
he should sweep streets even as
Michelangelo painted, or
Beethoven composed music, or
Shakespeare wrote poetry. He
should sweep streets so well that all
the hosts of heaven and earth will
pause to say, here lived a great
streetsweeper who did his job well.*

Martin Luther King, Jr.

There is a better way for
everything. Find it.

Thomas Edison

In his later years Pablo Picasso was
not allowed to roam an art gallery
unattended, for he had previously
been discovered in the act of trying
to improve on one of his old
masterpieces.

Anonymous

There is always room at the top.

Daniel Webster

Unless you try to do something
beyond what you have already
mastered you will never grow.

Ronald E. Osborn

Reach beyond your grasp. Your
goals should be grand enough to
get the best of you.

Pierre Teilhard de Chardin

The superior man is modest in his
speech but exceeds in his actions.

Confucius

A total commitment is paramount
to reaching the ultimate in
performance.

Tom Flores

Men must be decided on what they
will not do, and then they are able
to act with vigor on what they
ought to do.

Mencius

Much good work is lost for the lack
of a little more.

Edward Knight

To do the right thing, at the right time, in the right way; to do some things better than they were ever done before; to eliminate errors; to know both sides of the question; to be courteous; to be an example; to work for the love of work; to anticipate requirements; to develop resources; to recognize no impediments; to master circumstances; to act from reason rather than rule; to be satisfied with nothing short of perfection.

Marshall Field & Company

Happy are those who dream
dreams and are willing to pay the
price to make them come true.

Anonymous

Strategy is a style of thinking, a
conscious and deliberate process,
an intensive implementation
system, the science of insuring
future success.

Pete Johnson

All glory comes from daring to
begin.

Eugene F. Ware

My philosophy is that not only are
you responsible for your life, but
doing the best at this moment puts
you in the best place for the next
moment.

Oprah Winfrey

All successful employers are
stalking men who will do the
unusual, men who think, men who
attract attention by performing
more than is expected of them.

Charles Schwab

Enthusiasm is the mother of effort, and without it nothing great was ever achieved.

Ralph Waldo Emerson

A ship in port is safe, but that is not what ships are for. Sail out to sea and do new things.

Grace Hopper

Great achievement is usually born of great sacrifice, and is never the result of selfishness.

Napoleon Hill

Excellence is an art won by training and habituation. We do not act rightly because we have virtue or excellence, but we rather have those because we have acted rightly. We are what we repeatedly do. Excellence, then, is not an act but a habit.

Aristotle

You become a champion by fighting one more round. When things are tough, you fight one more round.

James Corbett

Act honestly, and answer boldly.

Danish proverb

The intelligent man is one who has successfully fulfilled many accomplishments, and is yet willing to learn more.

Ed Parker

A wise man will make more
opportunities than he finds.

Francis Bacon

Our goals can only be reached
through a vehicle of a plan, in
which we must fervently believe,
and upon which we must
vigorously act. There is no other
route to success.

Stephen A. Brennan

Diligence is the mother of good
luck.

Ben Franklin

Everyone should carefully observe
which way his heart draws him,
and then choose that way with all
his strength.

Jewish proverb

Genius begins great works; labor
alone finishes them.

Joseph Joubert

Those who attain any excellence
commonly spend life in one
pursuit; for excellence is not often
granted upon easier terms.

Samuel Johnson

Commitment
to Excellence

No one ever attains very
eminent success by simply
doing what is required of him;
it is the amount and excellence
of what is over and above the
required that determines the
greatness of ultimate distinction.

Charles Kendall Adams

Every success is built on the ability
to do better than good enough.

Anonymous

Success is the maximum utilization
of the ability you have.

Zig Ziglar

The man who goes farthest is
generally the one who is willing to
do and dare. The sure-thing boat
never gets far from shore.

Dale Carnegie

Commitment
to Excellence

Do your work; not just your work and no more, but a little more for the lavishing's sake—that little more which is worth all the rest.

Dean Briggs

The biggest temptation is to settle for too little.

Thomas Merton

Flaming enthusiasm, backed up by horse sense and persistence, is the quality that most frequently makes for success.

Dale Carnegie

No bird soars too high, if he soars
with his own wings.

William Blake

Excellence is rarely found, more
rarely valued.

Goethe

If something is exceptionally well
done it has embedded in its very
existence the aim of lifting the
common denominator rather than
catering to it.

Edward Fischer

If you are serious about your goals, drop the conditions. Go directly to your goal. Be your goal! Conditions often disguise strategies for escaping accountability. Why not just take charge and create the experience you are looking for?

Eric Allenbaugh

Courage to start and willingness
to keep everlasting at it are the
requisites for success.

Alonzo Newton Benn

The world steps aside for the man
who knows where he is going.

Anonymous

Be everywhere, do everything, and
never fail to astonish the customer.

Macy's Department Store

You can always find the sun within
yourself if you will only search.

Maxwell Maltz

They can conquer who believe
they can.

Virgil

It is not enough to do your best;
you must know what to do, and
then do your best.

W. Edwards Deming

No one ever gets far unless he
accomplishes the impossible at
least once a day.

Elbert Hubbard

The impossible is often the
untried.

Jim Goodwin

Excellence implies more than
competence—it implies a striving
for the highest possible standards.

Anonymous

Don't reserve your best behavior for special occasions. You can't have two sets of manners, two social codes—one for those you admire and want to impress, another for those whom you consider unimportant. You must be the same to all people.

Lillian Eichler Watson

Strength does not come from physical capacity. It comes from indomitable will.

Jawaharlal Nehru

Just keep doing. Everybody gets better if they keep at it.

Ted Williams

Keep your head and your heart going in the right direction and you will not have to worry about your feet.

Anonymous

Destiny is not a matter of chance, it is a matter of choice; it is not a thing to be waited for, it is a thing to be achieved.

William Jennings Bryan

Faith that the thing can be done is essential to any great achievement.

Thomas N. Carruther

I know the price of success: dedication, hard work, and a devotion to the things you want to see happen.

Frank Lloyd Wright

Four short words sum up what has lifted most successful individuals above the crowd: a little bit more.

A. Lou Vickery

Nothing great was ever achieved without enthusiasm.

Ralph Waldo Emerson

The ambitious climbs high and perilous stairs and never cares how to come down; the desire of rising hath swallowed up his fear of the fall.

Thomas Adams

The man who is anybody and
who does anything is going to
be criticized, vilified, and
misunderstood. That is part of
the penalty for greatness, and
every great man understands it;
and understands, too, that it is
no proof of greatness. The final
proof of greatness lies in being
able to endure continuously
without resentment.

Elbert Hubbard

The destiny of man is not
perfection, but growth.

Anonymous

Character cannot be developed in
ease and quiet. Only through
experience of trial and suffering
can the soul be strengthened,
vision cleared, ambition inspired,
and success achieved.

Helen Keller

The will to win is important, but
the will to prepare is vital.

Joe Paterno

Success seems to be largely a
matter of hanging on after others
have let go.

William Feather

They who are the most persistent,
and work in the true spirit, will
invariably be the most successful.

Samuel Smiles

Let me tell you the secret that has
led me to my goal. My strength lies
solely in my tenacity.

Louis Pasteur

Success based on anything but internal fulfillment is bound to be empty.

Dr. Martha Friedman

You can only become a winner if you are willing to walk over the edge.

Ronald E. McNair

No great thing comes to any man unless he has courage.

Cardinal James Gibbons

To do something better, you must work an extra bit harder. I like the phrase an extra bit harder. For me it is not just a slogan, but a habitual state of mind, a disposition. Any job one takes on must be grasped and felt with one's soul, mind, and heart; only then will one work an extra bit harder.

Mikhail Gorbachev

The only way to the top is by
persistent, intelligent, hard work.

A. T. Mercier

My motto was always to keep
swinging. Whether I was in a
slump or feeling badly or having
trouble off the field, the only thing
to do was keep swinging.

Hank Aaron

The mind is not a vessel to be filled
but a fire to be kindled.

Plutarch

No one reaches a high position
without daring.

Syrus

Perseverance is a great element of
success. If you only knock long
enough and loud enough at the
gate, you are sure to wake up
somebody.

Henry Wadsworth Longfellow

It is a rough road that leads to the
heights of greatness.

Seneca

I'm a great believer in luck, and I find the harder I work, the more I have of it.

Thomas Jefferson

Besides pride, loyalty, discipline, heart, and mind, confidence is the key to all the locks.

Joe Paterno

Excellence is available to all who are willing to make the commitment.

Byrd Baggett

My mother drew a distinction between achievement and success. She said that achievement is the knowledge that you have studied and worked hard and done the best that is in you. Success is being praised by others, and that's nice, too, but not as important or satisfying.

Helen Hayes

Success is to be measured not so much by the position that one has reached in life as by the obstacles which he has overcome while trying to succeed.

Booker T. Washington

If you set a goal for yourself and are able to achieve it, you have won your race. Your goal can be to come in first, to improve your performance, or just finish the race—it's up to you.

Dave Scott

He who stops being better stops
being good.

Oliver Cromwell

I've always made a total effort,
even when the odds seemed
entirely against me. I never quit
trying; I never felt I didn't have a
chance to win.

Arnold Palmer

Other people may not have had
high expectations for me, but I
had high expectations for myself.

Shannon Miller

The principle is competing against yourself. It's about self-improvement, about being better than you were the day before.

Steve Young

The more I train, the more I realize I have more speed in me.

Leroy Burrell

Genius is one percent inspiration and ninety-nine percent perspiration.

Thomas Edison

The true spirit of delight,
the exaltation, the sense of
being more than man, which
is the touchstone of the highest
excellence, is to be found in
mathematics as surely as
poetry.

Bertrand Russell

Character is higher than intellect.
A great soul will be strong to live as
well as think.

Ralph Waldo Emerson

Every production of genius must
be the production of enthusiasm.

Benjamin Disraeli

Great minds must be ready not
only to take opportunities, but to
make them.

Charles Caleb Colton

Commitment
to Excellence

The person who makes a success of living is the one who sees his goal steadily and aims for it unswervingly. That is dedication.

Cecil B. DeMille

Set your goals high, and don't stop till you get there.

Bo Jackson

Accept the challenges, so that you may feel the exhilaration of victory.

George S. Patton

Don't be afraid to take a big step if one is indicated. You can't cross a chasm in two small jumps.

David Lloyd George

Paralyze resistance with persistence.

Woody Hayes

A man sooner or later discovers that he is the master-gardener of his soul, the director of his life.

James Allen

The greatness comes not when things go always good for you. But the greatness comes when you're really tested, when you take some knocks, some disappointments, when sadness comes. Because only if you've been in the deepest valley can you ever know how magnificent it is to be on the highest mountain.

Richard Nixon

The first and best victory is to conquer self.

Plato

I've never sought success in order to get fame and money; It's the talent and the passion that count in success.

Ingrid Bergman

Don't bother about genius. Don't worry about being clever. Trust hard work, perseverance, and determination.

Sir Frederick Treves

Commitment
to Excellence

Do not anticipate trouble, or worry about what may never happen. Keep in the sunlight.

Benjamin Franklin

Infinite striving to be the best is man's duty, it is its own reward.

Gandhi

The most powerful factors in the world are clear ideas in the minds of energetic men of goodwill.

J. Arthur Thomson

Our thoughts and imaginations
are the only real limits to our
possibilities.

Orison Swett Marden

The actions of men are the best
interpreters of their thoughts.

John Locke

Little minds are tamed and
subdued by misfortune; but great
minds rise above them.

Washington Irving

The best advisors, helpers and friends, always are not those who tell us how to act in special cases, but who give us, out of themselves, the ardent spirit and desire to act right, and leave us then, even though many blunders, to find out what our own form of right action is.

Phillips Brooke

The difference between the
impossible and the possible lies
in a man's determination.

Tommy Lasorda

Let us train our minds to desire
what the situation demands.

Seneca

The best portion of a good man's
life is his little, nameless,
unremembered acts of kindness
and of love.

William Wordsworth

No pain, no palm; no thorns, no
throne; no gall, no glory; no cross,
no crown.

William Penn

A man's life is what his thoughts
make it.

Marcus Aurelius

The secret of greatness is simple:
do better work than any other man
in your field—and keep doing it.

Wilfred A. Peterson

The price of greatness is
responsibility.

Winston Churchill

No great man ever complains of
want of opportunity.

Ralph Waldo Emerson

Success is not so much
achievement as achieving. Refuse
to join the cautious crowd that
plays not to lose; play to win.

David J. Mahoney

At the root of human responsibility is the concept of perfection, the urge to achieve it, the intelligence to find a path towards it, and the will to follow that path, if not to the end at least the distance needed to rise above individual limitations and environmental impediments.

Aung San Suu Kyi

Every human mind is a great
slumbering power until awakened
by a keen desire and by definite
resolution to do.

Edgar F. Roberts

From now on, any definition of a
successful life must include serving
others.

George Bush

Your success will always be
measured by the quality and
quantity of service you render.

Earl Nightingale

Don't be afraid to give up the good to go for the great.

Kenny Rogers

We do not do well except when we know where the best is and when we are assured that we have touched it and hold its power within us.

Joseph Joubert

We must do the best we can with what we have.

Edward Rowland Sill

It isn't by size that you win or
fail—be the best of whatever you
are.

Douglas Malloch

Every successful man I have heard
of has done the best he could with
the conditions as he found them.

Edgar W. Howe

To succeed, it is necessary to accept
the world as it is and rise above it.

Michael Korda

Quality is never an accident.
It is always the result of high
intention, sincere effort,
intelligent direction, and
skillful execution; it represents
the wise choice of many
alternatives.

Willa A. Foster

I do not know anyone who has gotten to the top without hard work. That is the recipe. It will not always get you to the top, but it should get you pretty near.

Margaret Thatcher

The lights of stars that were extinguished ages ago still reach us. So it is with great men who died centuries ago, but still reach us with the radiations of their personalities.

Kahlil Gibran

Whenever a man does the best he can, then that is all he can do.

Harry S Truman

I want to be all that I am capable of becoming.

Katherine Mansfield

Surely a man has come to himself only when he has found the best that is in him, and he has satisfied his heart with the highest achievement he is fit for.

Woodrow Wilson

Effort is a commitment to seeing a task through to the end, not just until you get tired of it.

Howard Cato

Luck is a dividend of sweat. The more you sweat the luckier you get.

Ray Kroc

It's not necessarily the amount of time you spend at practice that counts; it's what you put into the practice.

Eric Lindros

*Few will have the greatness
to bend history itself; but each
of us can work to change a
small portion of events, and
in the total of all those acts
will be written the history of
this generation.*

Robert F. Kennedy

Your chances of success in any undertaking can always be measured by your belief in yourself.

Robert Collier

Never, ever, accept mediocrity.

Anonymous

I never knew a man come to greatness or eminence who lay abed late in the morning.

Jonathon Swift

I can't imagine a person becoming
a success who doesn't give this
game of life everything he's got.

Walter Cronkite

Everybody can be great, because
anybody can serve.

Martin Luther King, Jr.

You can do what you have to do,
and sometimes you can do it even
better than you think you can.

Jimmy Carter

The higher you soar the more beautiful the view.

Byrd Baggett

The road to excellence rarely has traffic.

Anonymous

To develop ease and confidence in doing, you must develop abilities and then develop excellence in the use of these abilities.

Rhoda Lachar

The best thing to give your enemy is forgiveness; to an opponent, tolerance; to a friend, your heart; to your child, a good example; to a father, deference; to your mother, conduct that will make her proud of you; to yourself, respect; to all men, charity.

Francis Maitland Balfour

In golf, as in life, perfection is an unattainable goal. Be the best you can be. That is enough.

Leonard Finkel

He is not great who is not greatly good.

William Shakespeare

Keep away from people who try to belittle your ambitions. Small people always do that, but the really great make you feel that you, too, can become great.

Mark Twain

Commitment
to Excellence

Do what you know best; if you are a
runner, run, if you're a bell, ring.

Ignas Bernstein

If you would attain greatness, think
no little thoughts.

Anonymous

It is not the greatness of a
man's means that makes him
independent, so much as the
smallness of his wants.

William Cobbett

By constant self-discipline and self-control you can develop greatness of character.

Grenville Kleiser

Great men are the guideposts and landmarks in the state.

Edmund Burke

Success seems to be connected with action. Successful men keep moving. They make mistakes, but they don't quit.

Conrad Hilton

We *distinguish the excellent*
man from the common man
by saying that the former is
the one who makes great
demands on himself, and the
latter who makes no demands
on himself.

Jose Ortega y Gasset

I never wanted to set records. The only thing I strived for was perfection.

Wilt Chamberlain

A man dies when he refuses to stand up for that which is right. A man dies when he refuses to take a stand for that which is true.

Martin Luther King, Jr.

Always do your best. What you plant now, you will harvest later.

Og Mandino

Commitment
to Excellence

It's amazing what ordinary people
can do if they set out without
preconceived notions.

Charles F. Kettering

Even if you're on the right track,
you'll get run over if you just sit
there.

Will Rogers

I do not try to dance better than
anyone else. I only try to dance
better than myself.

Mikhail Baryshnikov

All our dreams can come true, if
we have the courage to pursue
them.

Walt Disney

Success is the result of perfection,
hard work, learning from failure,
loyalty, and persistence.

Colin Powell

You don't start climbing a
mountain to get to the middle.
Why be content with being
average?

James Hart

I *believe that any man's life will be filled with constant and unexpected encouragement, if he makes up his mind to do his level best each day, and as nearly as possible reaching the high water mark of pure and useful living.*

Booker T. Washington

The achievement of your goal is
assured the moment you commit
yourself to it.

Mack R. Douglas

Make the best use of what is in
your power, and take the rest as it
happens.

Epictetus

You get the best out of others when
you get the best out of yourself.

Harvey Firestone

Commitment
to Excellence

You better live your best and act
your best and think your best
today, for today is the sure
preparation for tomorrow and all
the other tomorrows that follow.

Harriet Marineau

A problem is a chance for you to
do your best.

Duke Ellington

Only the mediocre are always at
their best.

Jean Giraudoux

Genius is nothing but continued
attention.

Claude A. Helvetius

The individual must not merely
wait and criticize, he must defend
the cause the best he can. The fate
of the world will be such as the
world deserves.

Albert Einstein

Practice is the best of all
instructors.

Syrus

People are always blaming their circumstances for what they are. I don't believe in circumstances. The people who get on in this world are the people who get up and look for the circumstances they want, and if they can't find them, make them.

George Bernard Shaw

The best and most beautiful things
in the world cannot be seen or
even touched. They must be felt.

Helen Keller

The best way to have a good idea is
to have a lot of ideas.

Dr. Linus Pauling

No man is truly great who is great
only in his lifetime. The test of
greatness is the page of history.

William Hazlitt

The ripest peach is highest on the tree.

James Whitcomb Riley

Greatness, in the last analysis, is largely bravery—courage in escaping from old ideas and old standards and respectable ways of doing things.

James Harvey Robinson

No one has a corner on success. It is his who pays the price.

Orison Swett Marden

It had long since come to my attention that people of accomplishment rarely sat back and let things happen to them. They went out and happened to things.

Elinor Smith

We write our own destiny. We become what we do.

Madame Chiang Kai-Shek

What is called genius is the abundance of life and health.

Henry David Thoreau

B*ecome a possibilitarian.*
No matter how dark things
seem to be or actually are,
raise your sights and see the
possibilities—always see them,
for they're always there.

Norman Vincent Peale

I just go out and do the best that I can do.

Wilson Alvarez

Always remember what you're good at and stick with it.

Ermenegildo Zegna

I'm the foe of moderation, the champion of excess. If I may lift a line from a diehard whose identity is lost in the shuffle, I'd rather be strongly wrong than weakly right.

Tallulah Bankhead

Commitment
to Excellence

We will be victorious if we have not forgotten to learn.

Rosa Luxemburg

You have to learn the rules of the game. And then you have to play better than anyone else.

Dianne Feinstein

The measure of a truly great man is the courtesy with which he treats lesser men.

Anonymous

We must dare, and dare again, and go on daring.

Georges Jacques Danton

You do what you can for as long as you can, and when you finally can't, you do the next best thing. You back up but you don't give up.

Chuck Yeager

As long as you're going to think anyway, think big.

Donald Trump

It is folly for an eminent person
to think of escaping censure, and
a weakness to be affected by it.
All the illustrious persons of
antiquity, and indeed of every age,
have passed through this fiery
persecution. There is no defense
against reproach but obscurity;
it is a kind of concomitant to
greatness, as satires and invectives
were an essential part of a Roman
triumph.

Joseph Addison

Nothing liberates our greatness
like the desire to help, the desire to
serve.

Marianne Williamson

Don't bunt. Aim out of the ball
park. Aim for the company of the
immortals.

David Ogilvy

Pride is a personal commitment.
It is an attitude that separates
excellence from mediocrity.

Anonymous

Be bold. If you're going to make
an error, make a doozy, and don't
be afraid to hit the ball.

Billie Jean King

You can be an ordinary athlete
by getting away with less than
your best. But if you want to be a
great, you have to give it all you've
got—your everything.

Duke P. Kahanamoku

Striving for excellence motivates
you.

Dr. Harriet Braiker

Whatever I engage in, I must push inordinately.

Andrew Carnegie

People need to feel better about themselves, to feel that, yes, they can do it. First you think highly of yourself; then you accelerate.

Janet Norflett

To succeed in any endeavor takes relentless belief in yourself. We have to be committed. We can determine our destiny.

Willie B. White

To dream anything that you want to dream. That is the beauty of the humankind. To do anything that you want to do. That is the strength of human will. To trust yourself to test your limits. That is the courage to succeed.

Bernard Edmonds

I never wanted to be famous. I
only wanted to be great.

Ray Charles

Success is not achieved by working
until the whistle sounds at the end
of the day but by working even
though the whistle has sounded at
the end of the day.

Roderick Van Murchison

Keep company with those who may
make you better.

English proverb

It's amazing how close to
perfection you can get if you're
willing to try.

Anonymous

It's very important to define
success for yourself. If you really
want to reach for the brass ring,
just remember that there are
sacrifices that go along.

Cathleen Black

Greatness does not approach him
who is forever looking down.

Hitopadesa

Unless you try to do something
beyond what you have already
mastered, you will never grow.

Ronald E. Osborn

The quality of a person's life is
in direct proportion to their
commitment to excellence,
regardless of their chosen field
of endeavor.

Vince Lombardi

Small minds are the first to
condemn great ideas.

Anonymous

Success attracts success! There is no escape from this great universal law; therefore, if you wish to attract success make sure that you look the part of success, whether your calling is that of a day laborer or a merchant prince.

Napoleon Hill

Resolve to make each day the very best and don't let anyone get in your way. If they do, step on them.

Ivan Benson

Choice, not chance, determines destiny.

Anonymous

I have always had a drive that pushed me to try for perfection, and golf is a game in which perfection stays just out of reach.

Betsy Rawls

The quality of expectations
determines the quality of our
action.

Andre Godin

The real contest is always between
what you've done and what you're
capable of doing. You measure
yourself against yourself and
nobody else.

Geoffrey Gaberino

Always do more than is expected of
you.

George S. Patton

You have to create a track record
of breaking your own mold, or at
least other people's idea of that
mold.

William Hurt

To succeed, do the best you can,
where you are, with what you have.

Anonymous

The uncommon man is merely
the common man thinking and
dreaming of success in larger terms
and in more fruitful areas.

Melvin Powers

What is the recipe for successful achievement? To my mind there are just four essential ingredients: Choose a career you love. Give it the best there is in you. Seize your opportunities. And be a member of the team.

Benjamin F. Fairless

It is constant effort to be first-class
in everything one attempts that
conquers the heights of excellence.

Orison Swett Marden

Ingenuity, plus courage, plus work,
equals miracles.

Bob Richards

It is a funny thing about life: If you
refuse to accept anything but the
very best, you will very often get it.

W. Somerset Maugham

Commitment
to Excellence

To fight and conquer in all your battles is not supreme excellence; supreme excellence consists in breaking the enemy's resistance without fighting.

Sun Tzu

It is our duty as men and women to proceed as though the limits of our abilities do not exist.

Pierre Teilhard de Chardin

I never had a policy; I have just tried to do my very best each and every day.

Abraham Lincoln

Do not follow where the path may
lead. Go instead where there is no
path and leave a trail.

Anonymous

Nothing can resist the human will
that will stake even its existence on
its stated purpose.

Benjamin Disraeli

If we want to make something
really superb on this planet,
there is nothing whatever that
can stop us.

Shepherd Mead

I *believe that the first test of a truly great man is his humility. I don't mean by humility, doubt of his power. But really great men have a curious feeling that the greatness is not of them, but through them. And they see something divine in every other man and are endlessly, foolishly, incredibly merciful.*

John Ruskin

There are only two options
regarding commitment. You're
either *in* or you're *out*. There's no
such thing as life in-between.

Pat Riley

I've always tried to go a step past
wherever people expected me to
end up.

Beverly Sills

The roots of true achievement lie
in the will to become the best that
you can become.

Harold Taylor

Great spirits have always
encountered violent opposition
from mediocre minds.

Albert Einstein

Power is not revealed by striking
hard or often, but by striking true.

Honoré de Balzac

Far and away the best prize that life
offers is the chance to work hard at
work worth doing.

Theodore Roosevelt

If better is possible, good is not
enough.

Anonymous

Demand the best from yourself,
because others will demand the
best of you. Successful people don't
simply give a project hard work.
They give it their best work.

Win Borden

Actually, all I ever wanted to be was
the best in my field.

Lou Holtz

Desire is the key to motivation, but it's the determination and commitment to an unrelenting pursuit of your goal—a commitment to excellence—that will enable you to attain the success you seek.

Mario Andretti

High aims form high characters,
and great objectives bring out
great minds.

Anonymous

Reach high, for the stars lie hidden
in your soul. Dream deep, for
every dream precedes the goal.

Pamela Vaull Starr

Honesty is the best image.

Tom Wilson, "Ziggy"

The progress of the world is the history of men who would not permit defeat to speak the final word.

J. R. Sizoo

In every thought and action, think excellence.

Byrd Baggett

Champion the right to be yourself; dare to be different and set your own pattern; live your life and follow your own star.

Anonymous

Our imagination is the only limit
to what we can hope to have in the
future.

Charles Kettering

The secret of genius is to carry the
spirit of the child into old age,
which means never losing your
enthusiasm.

Aldous Huxley

The dedicated life is the life worth
living. You must give with your
whole heart.

Annie Dillard

To be nobody-but-yourself
in a world which is doing its
best, night and day, to make
you everybody else—means to
fight the hardest battle which
any human being can fight;
and never stop fighting.

e.e. cummings

If you can imagine it, you can achieve it. If you can dream it, you can become it.

William Arthur Ward

Great men are rarely isolated mountain-peaks; they are the summits of ranges.

Thomas Wentworth Higginson

Never go backward. Attempt, and do it with all your might. Determination is power.

Charles Simmons

The spirit, the will to win, and the will to excel are the things that endure. These qualities are so much more important than the events that occur.

Vince Lombardi

Shoot for the moon. Even if you miss it you will land among the stars.

Anonymous

Good enough never is.

Debbi Fields

You really can change the world if you care enough.

Marian Wright Edelman

Excellence is best described as doing the right things right—selecting the most important things to be done and then accomplishing them 100% correctly.

Anonymous

I want to be great, something special.

Sugar Ray Leonard

To laugh often and much; to win the respect of intelligent people and the affection of children; to earn the appreciation of honest critics and endure the betrayal of false friends; to appreciate beauty; to find the best in others; to leave the world a bit better, whether by a healthy child, a garden patch, a redeemed social condition; to know even one life has breathed easier because you have lived. This is to have succeeded.

Ralph Waldo Emerson

You have to invest yourself. There are no nine-to-five possibilities in terms of true success in business or the professions. Dedication is the key.

Jack Hilton

Act as though it were impossible to fail.

Anonymous

One man has enthusiasm for 30 minutes, another for 30 days, but it is the man what has it for 30 years who makes a success of his life.

Edward B. Butler

Every job is a self-portrait of the person who did it. Autograph your work with excellence.

Anonymous

There is no challenge more challenging than improving yourself.

Michael Staley

If you want to succeed you should strike out on new paths rather than travel the worn paths of accepted success.

John D. Rockefeller

These other Successories® titles are available from Career Press:

➤ *The Magic of Motivation*

➤ *The Essence of Attitude*

➤ *The Power of Goals*

➤ *Winning with Teamwork*

➤ *The Best of Success*

To order call: 1-800-CAREER-1

These other Successories® titles are available from Career Press:

➤ *Great Little Book on The Gift of Self-Confidence*

➤ *Great Little Book on The Peak Performance Woman*

➤ *Great Little Book on Mastering Your Time*

➤ *Great Little Book on Effective Leadership*

➤ *Great Little Book on Personal Achievement*

➤ *Great Little Book on Successful Selling*

➤ *Great Little Book on Universal Laws of Success*

➤ *Great Quotes from Great Women*

➤ *Great Quotes from Great Sports Heroes*

➤ *Great Quotes from Great Leaders*

➤ *Great Quotes from Zig Ziglar*

To order call: 1-800-CAREER-1